This Little Tiger book belongs to:

Fidgety Fish
and Friends

Ruth Galloway

written by Paul Bright

LITTLE TIGER PRESS
London

swoosh!

FIDGETY FISH

I love to flap and fidget,

To dive and dart and dash.

I wiggle my bottom and jiggle my tail,

With a fidgety splish, splosh, splash!

SMILEY SHARK

All sensible sharks agree,

I'm silly as a shark can be.

I giggle and grin if you tickle my fin,

And wiggle my tail with glee.

AMAZING ANGELFISH

There are short fish, long fish, thin fish, fat fish,

Funny-looking flatfish, dogfish, catfish.

Some are very big, some are teeny-weeny small.

Can I be the one who is the prettiest of all?

CLICKETY CRAB

My snip-snap claws go clickety-click,
My toes tap a tune on the sand.
I drum on my tum and I whistle and hum,
I'm the wonderful one-crab band!

SNIP-SNAP!

CLICKETY-CLICK!

Hello!

SHY OCTOPUS
Octopus hides inside his cave,
He's really rather shy.
So please give him a friendly wave,
Next time you're passing by.

JIGGLY JELLYFISH

We wibble and we wobble,
Like jelly in a dish.

WHOOSH!

SWIRLY STARFISH

We are the wonderful starfish,

We swirl and we scamper about.

We skip and we spin as the tide's coming in,

Then again as the tide's going out.

SHINY SNAILS

Shiny, tiny sea snails,
Sliding on the rocks.
They don't have any feet,
So they don't need any socks!

SUPER SEAHORSES

Can you see the seahorses? Can you spot a snout?

Can you find a tail, or a tummy sticking out?

Can you see the seahorse friends, all playing peek-a-boo?

Jumping out and laughing, shouting, "I've found you!"

PROUD PUFFERFISH

Why does a pufferfish puff! puff! puff!

Only the pufferfish knows.

He blows out his chest with a huff! huff! huff!

And grows and grows and grows!

TERRIFIC TURTLE

See the fishes join the fun
When turtle comes to play.
Chasing, hiding, swooshing, gliding,
Laughing all the way.

FIDGETY FISH AND FRIENDS

Swimming and skittering under the sea,

With a smile and a swirl and a swish.

All of his friends love to play every day

With the fabulous Fidgety Fish!

LITTLE TIGER PRESS
An imprint of Magi Publications
1 The Coda Centre, 189 Munster Road, London SW6 6AW
www.littletigerpress.com

First published in Great Britain 2008
This edition published 2008

A CIP catalogue record for this book is available from the British Library

Printed in China

2 4 6 8 10 9 7 5 3

Make friends with all these books from Little Tiger Press

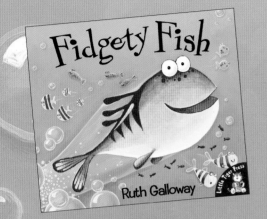

Fidgety Fish
Ruth Galloway

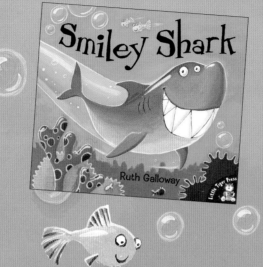

Smiley Shark
Ruth Galloway

Clumsy Crab
Ruth Galloway

IT'S TIME TO SLEEP, **YOU CRAZY SHEEP!**
Alison Ritchie
Illustrated by Cornelia Haas

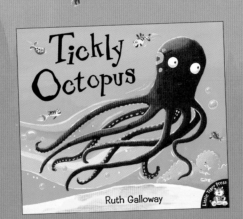

Tickly Octopus
Ruth Galloway

QUIET!
Paul Bright
Illustrated by Guy Parker-Rees

For information regarding any of the above titles
or for our catalogue, please contact us:
Little Tiger Press, 1 The Coda Centre,
189 Munster Road, London SW6 6AW
Tel: 020 7385 6333 Fax: 020 7385 7333
E-mail: info@littletiger.co.uk www.littletigerpress.com